For Louis

First U.S. edition 1995

Library of Congress Cataloging-in-Publication Data

McDonnell, Flora.
I love boats / by Flora McDonnell.
Summary: A little girl lists all the boats she loves most
and plays with in the bath.
ISBN 1-56402-539-X
1. Boats and boating—Fiction.   [1. Baths— Fiction.]   I. Title.
PZ7.M478434Iaac   1995
[E]—dc20   94-4861

10 9 8 7 6 5 4 3 2

Printed in Hong Kong

The pictures in this book were done in
acrylic and gouache.

Candlewick Press
2067 Massachusetts Avenue
Cambridge, Massachusetts 02140

I Love Boats

Flora McDonnell

CANDLEWICK PRESS
CAMBRIDGE, MASSACHUSETTS

I love the old boat
being painted
red and green.

I love the houseboat

with a family on board.

I love
the
dredger

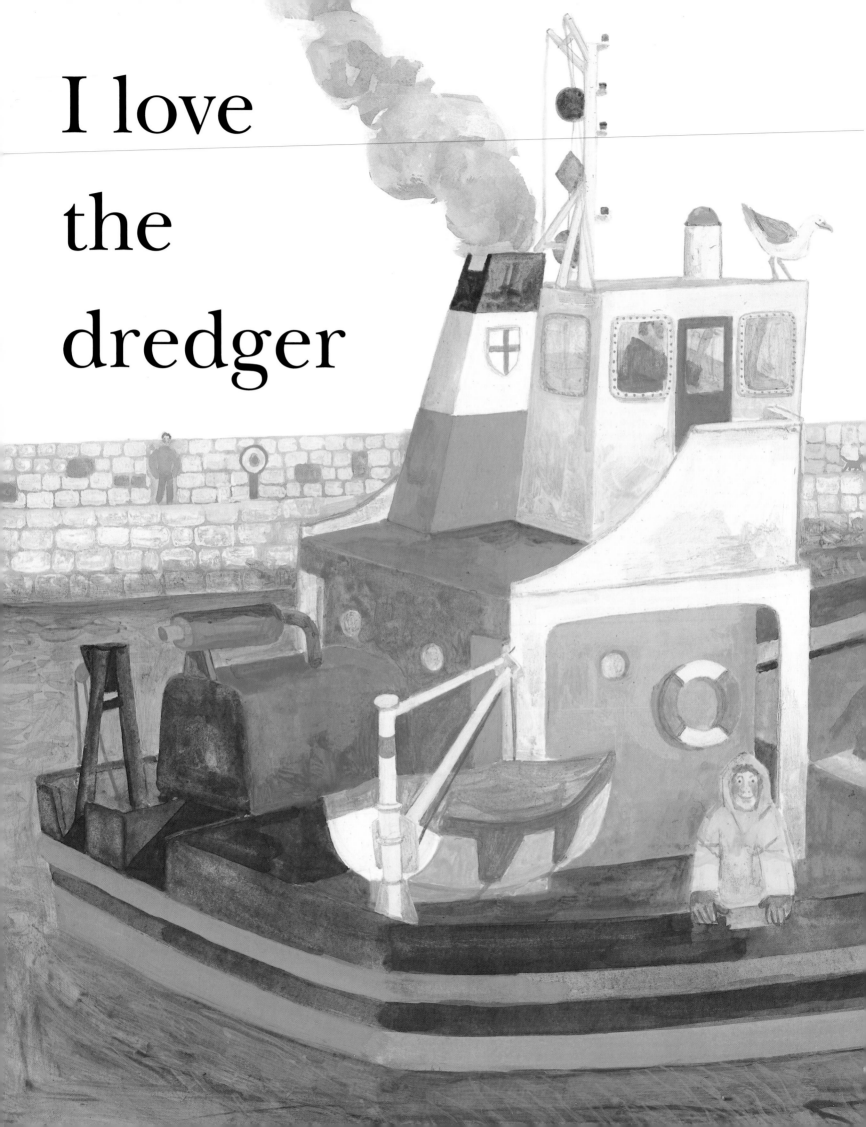

scooping
up the
mud.

I love the lobster boat

bobbing on the waves.

I love the ferry loading up with cars.

I love the cargo boat with lots of crates on deck.

I love the tug towing a big ship out to sea.

I love the liner
far out on the ocean.

I love the
sailboat

speeding with the wind.

I love the
rowing boats

racing around the rock.

I love the trawlers bringing home the fish.

I love *all* the boats

floating in my bath.

Blackbeard's Last Fight

Eric A. Kimmel
Pictures by **Leonard Everett Fisher**

Farrar, Straus and Giroux

New York

Jeremy Hobbs's heels clicked on the polished oak floor as he
followed Lieutenant Maynard down the hallway. The stiff, buckled
shoes pinched his toes. As cabin boy on the HMS *Pearl*, Jeremy went
barefoot most of the time. Stern, bewigged gentlemen glowered from
portraits on the walls.

"Governors of Virginia, all the way back to John Smith, I daresay,"
the lieutenant remarked, as much at ease in the Governor's House as on the
Pearl's quarterdeck. "Tell Governor Spotswood that Lieutenant Maynard is
here to see him," he announced to the footman standing at the end of the
hallway. The footman bowed and disappeared behind a large door.

"Now, remember, Hobbs," Lieutenant Maynard whispered to Jeremy,
"Alexander Spotswood is a powerful man. It won't do to offend him in any
way. You're to stand close and say nothing. Above all, whatever you hear or
see remains secret."

"Aye, aye, sir!"

The door opened. Lieutenant Maynard saluted the stern, red-faced gentleman standing beside a table strewn with maps and papers. "Lieutenant Robert Maynard, Royal Navy." He took off his hat and handed it to Jeremy, who followed behind as if he were the lieutenant's shadow.

"Come in, Lieutenant. We have some serious matters to discuss. Can I count on your discretion?" the governor asked.

"Absolutely."

Governor Spotswood got to the point. "I assume that you are familiar with a certain seagoing ruffian known as Blackbeard."

Jeremy's eyes opened wide. Blackbeard was the most feared pirate in the colonies.

"Everyone knows that name, especially after what he did in Charleston," Lieutenant Maynard replied.

"An outrage!" Governor Spotswood's voice deepened with anger. "The rascal blockaded the port for a month. He looted ships and held honest citizens hostage. The people of Charleston had to pay an enormous ransom to get rid of him. And where was the Royal Navy?"

"The Navy cannot be everywhere at once. Our nearest man-o'-war was hundreds of miles away. I assure you, Governor, that if Blackbeard ever appears in Virginia's waters, we will deal with him."

"You may soon have the chance. These letters inform me that Blackbeard has settled in North Carolina, our neighbor to the south. By means fair or foul he has obtained a royal pardon from the governor. But that pirate can no more change his nature than a leopard can change her spots. It is clear that Blackbeard means to establish a base in Ocracoke Inlet. If he succeeds, those pirates will control the coast of North America."

The lieutenant paused before answering. "With due respect, Governor, a pardon is a pardon. Blackbeard's slate has been rubbed clean. Until he commits an act of piracy, as he did in Charleston, the Navy has no authority to send its ships against him. We couldn't do it, anyway. North Carolina's shifting channels are too shallow for a man-o'-war. It would be aground in a minute."

Governor Spotswood nodded. "I agree. Officially, my hands are tied. However, what if I hired my own ships? I would need a bold officer to lead a crew of sailors willing to take on a nest of pirates and wipe them out. For money, of course. The deed must be done before anyone learns of it. You come highly recommended."

Lieutenant Maynard did not hesitate to reply this time. "Governor, I am your man."

And I, too, thought Jeremy Hobbs.

The pale November sun began its descent as two ships, the *Jane* and the *Ranger*, flying England's flag of St. George's cross, sailed into the quiet waters of North Carolina's Ocracoke Inlet. They were sloops: single-masted maneuverable vessels able to navigate in shallow coastal waters where larger ships could not go. Sloops were ideal vessels for pirate hunters.

From the *Jane*, Lieutenant Maynard signaled to the *Ranger* to drop anchor.

"There she lies, beyond the dune." The lookout pointed toward the black flag flapping in the breeze.

The first mate squinted into the setting sun. "Aye! A skeleton hoisting an hourglass. That's Blackbeard's flag. We've found his ship, the *Adventure*."

Jeremy and the rest of the crew clustered at the rail for a look. They whispered the stories they had heard about Blackbeard.

"Rum mixed with gunpowder. 'Tis Blackbeard's favorite drink, so I hear. He sets it alight, then drinks the flaming brew in a gulp."

"Why do they call him Blackbeard?" Jeremy asked.

The first mate answered. "Because he has a beard like no other. It is as coarse as mattress stuffing. He braids it into little pigtails that he ties with ribbons."

"By the North Star! I'd like to see that!" Jeremy exclaimed.

"Would you, now? Aye, but that ain't all. Sometimes he'll set gunners' matches beneath his hat to light up his face and give him the look of a hellish fiend. But keep your distance. Blackbeard will shoot a man down for no reason at all. As he tells his crew, 'If I don't kill one of you now and then, you'll forget who I am.'"

"Why would his crew follow a captain who shoots them?"

"Because they love him," a sailor replied. "They're a rough lot. They know they need a firm hand."

"Aye, love him they do!" the mate agreed. "Especially the Africans Blackbeard set free. And the ladies! There's something about a rascal to set their hearts aflutter. I hear Blackbeard's been married fifteen times."

"Sixteen," the sailor said.

"Back to your posts!" Lieutenant Maynard commanded. "No need to talk about that rogue. We'll see enough of him on the morrow."

As the sky darkened, the cook passed out hardtack and strips of dried beef to those who felt like eating. Jeremy thought about the coming day and what it might bring. He knew that their mission was to wipe out Blackbeard and his crew. Even so, he couldn't help being fascinated by the man.

Lieutenant Maynard allowed no fires to be lit aboard the sloops that night. Still, he told the crew, the pirates had spies along the coast. They must surely know who these sailors were and why they had come.

Aboard the *Adventure* every light burned. The notes of a fiddle scraping out a tune to the beat of an African drum drifted across the water. Jeremy wondered what the pirates were planning. He was certain that Blackbeard was not afraid of anyone.

The first glint of dawn appeared above the eastern horizon. The incoming tide filtered through the reeds. Jeremy rubbed his eyes. He had passed a sleepless night. He and his shipmates gathered on the deck to receive their orders.

"Counting our crew and the *Ranger*'s, we outnumber the pirates three to one," said Lieutenant Maynard. "They have eight cannon aboard. We have only muskets and pistols. My hope is that the incoming tide will bring us alongside the *Adventure*. We'll keep up a steady fire to prevent her crew from manning the cannon, allowing us to board. Are you ready for a sea fight, lads?"

"Aye, aye!" replied the crew.

Jeremy gripped his cutlass. His mouth felt dry and his stomach tightened. He had never been in a sea battle before. He hoped he would act bravely.

Maynard signaled to the *Ranger* to raise the anchor and prepare for action.

At that moment the *Adventure* began to move. Silently, Lieutenant Maynard signaled to his sloops to follow Blackbeard into the narrow, twisting channel that ran between the dunes.

Jeremy saw a tall man with an enormous beard step to the rail. The pirate glared and shook his fist at the sloops. "Curse you for villains! Who are you? From whence came you?"

Lieutenant Maynard answered boldly. He raised his sword toward the ship's flag. "You may see by our colors that we are no pirates."

"Pass me up a bowl of rum," Blackbeard ordered his mate. He lifted the cup in a defiant toast to Maynard. "The devil seize my soul if I give you any quarter or take any from you."

"I expect no quarter from you. Nor shall I give any," Maynard answered.

No quarter! Jeremy knew that meant a fight to the death.

The *Jane* suddenly lurched. She had run aground on a hidden sandbar. The *Ranger*, trying to steer around her, ran aground, too.

The sloops had sailed into Blackbeard's trap. The pirates knew every inch of these shifting channels. The *Jane* and the *Ranger* were both stuck in the sand, unable to move, as the *Adventure* began to turn.

"Every man down! Take cover!" Maynard screamed to his crew.

Jeremy threw himself onto the deck. He heard Blackbeard roar, "Give them a broadside!"

Four cannon on the *Adventure*'s port side belched fire and smoke. A deadly hail of musket balls and bits of old iron shredded the sloops and their crews. Dying men littered the decks. But the tremendous recoil of the cannon pushed the *Adventure* onto the sand. Now all three ships lay aground.

Jeremy saw Lieutenant Maynard signaling to the *Ranger*. No answer came. With her mast down and most of her crew dead, the second sloop was out of the fight.

The *Jane* had lost half her crew, but the mast and the mainsail had survived the broadside. They had a chance—if they could get off the sandbar before the pirates did.

"The tide is still coming in," Maynard told his crewmen. "We may yet float, if we can lighten the ship. Broach the water casks! Overboard with the ballast! Hurry!"

"Aye, aye, Lieutenant!" said the first mate. Dazed, the crew ran to carry out the orders.

Jeremy stuck his cutlass in his belt. He helped throw boxes and barrels over the side.

The *Jane* shuddered. Her hull shifted as the incoming tide began lifting her out of the sand. The crew cheered.

"Silence!" Maynard ordered. "This fight's not over yet. One more broadside and we're finished. We must trick the pirates into thinking they have won."

He laid out his plan. Maynard and most of the survivors would hide belowdecks. Two sailors would remain at the helm to steer the *Jane* toward the *Adventure*. Maynard chose the two smallest. One was Jeremy.

"You're to steer, not fight. Use that cutlass only to defend yourself," Maynard ordered.

"Aye, aye, Lieutenant!" Jeremy replied.

Jeremy saw Blackbeard peering through the smoke. The pirate seemed to be smiling at the bodies of sailors scattered about the *Jane*'s deck like broken dolls.

Jeremy heard him give the order to attack. "Blast you!" Blackbeard roared at his crew. "Board her, and cut what's left of them to pieces!"

With grappling irons, the pirates pulled the ships together. They peppered the *Jane*'s deck with homemade grenades: bottles filled with gunpowder, bullets, and bits of metal.

Blackbeard drew his cutlass. Amid the noise and smoke, he leaped aboard. His pirates followed, brandishing cutlasses and pistols.

Jeremy grasped his own weapon as the pirates swarmed across the *Jane*'s deck. He felt too excited to be afraid. "Now! Have at them!" he heard Lieutenant Maynard shout.

The sailors poured out of the hold to attack the pirates. The *Jane*'s crew took them by surprise. But Blackbeard and his men fought back savagely.

No one could stand before Blackbeard. He wielded his cutlass like a scythe, cutting down every man in his path—until he came face-to-face with Jeremy.

Jeremy raised his own cutlass. Blackbeard knocked it from his hand. "I kill men, not boys!" he snarled. "Go hide belowdecks till this is over. You're a brave lad. I'll let you join my crew."

Jeremy heard a sudden shout. "Surrender, Blackbeard! Lay down your arms and I'll promise you a fair trial." It was Lieutenant Maynard. He stood behind Blackbeard, aiming a pistol.

Blackbeard turned. "Aye, and a fair hanging!" he sneered, pointing his pistol at Maynard.

The two pistols went off at once. Blackbeard missed, but Maynard's bullet, as big as a grape, struck the pirate in the chest.

Such a wound would have killed an ordinary man. But Blackbeard only laughed. "Have at you, you puppy!" he shouted. He threw his pistol aside and slashed at Maynard with his cutlass. Maynard parried the blow with his sword. The blade snapped in two. Blackbeard rushed in for the kill.

Jeremy snatched up the pirate's empty pistol. He leaped into the rigging and struck Blackbeard with the butt end. The pirate saluted Jeremy. "A good stroke, lad! Had you been bigger and stronger, you might have told your children that you toppled Blackbeard the pirate. But not quite!" He lunged at Maynard.

"Now, men! At him!" the lieutenant yelled.

The sailors attacked from all sides. Blackbeard snarled like a wolf at bay. He took a step forward—and fell dead on the deck.

The other pirates quickly surrendered. Jeremy helped lock them in irons. They would be brought back to Virginia to stand trial for their crimes.

As for Blackbeard, Maynard ordered his head cut off—beard, ribbons, and all—and hung from the *Jane*'s bowsprit. "We'll bring back a trophy such as Virginia has never seen!" he told his crew. "Blackbeard has received his just deserts."

The lieutenant was right, of course, but Blackbeard had spared Jeremy's life and done good for others. Jeremy knew in his heart that something terrible and fierce had gone from the world and that he would miss it.

The pirate's body was dropped overboard. The currents carried Blackbeard's headless corpse around the *Jane* three times. "He's looking for his head," a sailor murmured.

As the last remains of Blackbeard the pirate sank forever beneath the dark waters of Ocracoke Inlet, the corpse waved its right arm. Jeremy felt certain it was waving to him.

Author's Note

The legend of Blackbeard the pirate, whose real name may have been Edward Teach, lives on in North Carolina's Outer Banks. On Ocracoke Island, site of Blackbeard's headquarters, tourists can visit Teach's Hole, where he anchored his ship, and Teach's Oak, where he caroused with his crew in the days when Pamlico Sound appeared on maps as Pamticoe Sound. Close by are various places where he supposedly buried his treasure.

My main sources for this account of Blackbeard's last fight were Robert Earl Lee's *Blackbeard the Pirate*, David Cordingly's *Under the Black Flag*, and Captain Charles Johnson's *A General History of the Robberies and Murders of the Most Notorious Pyrates*. Captain Johnson was at one time identified as Daniel Defoe, the author of *Robinson Crusoe*. This theory now seems doubtful, and Captain Johnson remains a mystery. However, he certainly knew a great deal about pirate life; he may at one time have been a pirate himself.

Jeremy Hobbs is a fictional character, but the details of the battle are historically accurate. Surprisingly, Lieutenant Maynard's expedition was entirely illegal. Governor Spotswood had no right to send an armed force into a neighboring colony's waters to attack a peaceful citizen, no matter what his past. At the time of his death, Blackbeard was enjoying a full royal pardon.

To Captain Leonard —E.A.K.

To Richard Benjamin Fisher —L.E.F.

Text copyright © 2006 by Shearwater Books
Illustrations copyright © 2006 by Leonard Everett Fisher
All rights reserved
Distributed in Canada by Douglas & McIntyre Ltd.
Color separations by Chroma Graphics PTE Ltd.
Printed and bound in the United States of America by Berryville Graphics
Designed by Jay Colvin
First edition, 2006
1 3 5 7 9 10 8 6 4 2

www.fsgkidsbooks.com

Library of Congress Cataloging-in-Publication Data
Kimmel, Eric A.
    Blackbeard's last fight / Eric A. Kimmel ; pictures by Leonard Everett Fisher.— 1st ed.
        p. cm.
    Summary: In 1718, off the coast of North Carolina, a young cabin boy assists in the final capture and execution of Blackbeard the pirate.
    ISBN-13: 978-0-374-30780-6
    ISBN-10: 0-374-30780-6
    1. Teach, Edward, d. 1718—Juvenile fiction. [1. Blackbeard, d. 1718—Fiction. 2. Pirates—Fiction. 3. North Carolina—History—Colonial period, ca. 1600–1775—Fiction. 4. Virginia—History—Colonial period, ca. 1600–1775—Fiction.] I. Fisher, Leonard Everett, ill. II. Title.
PZ7.K5648Bl 2006
[Fic]—dc22

2003069365